Death's Romance

By

Danielle Wolfe

To my Dad, Timothy Mccomack.
To the men who stay by our side and become our 'Ride or Die'.

I love you.

Death's Romance Playlist

Infinity- James Young

Like that- Sleep Token

Afterlife- Evanesence

The Offering- Sleep Token

The Unforgiven- Metallica

Done with Everything- Line so Thin

Relic- Awaken I Am

is that love? – cloudyfield

Dangerous- Sleep Token

Arcade- Duncan Laurence

Emergence- Sleep Token

Gorgeous Nightmare- Escape the Fate

One for the Money- Escape the Fate

Collar of Truth- Violent Vira

Sweet Dreams- Marilyn Manson

Bulletproof-Godsmack

Roses-Awaken I Am
Wrong Side of Heaven- Five Finger Death Punch
Lifetime- Chris Grey

Scan for Death's Romance Playlist

PROLOGUE

Scan each QR code for a surprise
song

The paint around the altar slowly peels with each passing year. This has been my sanctuary ever since that day. I neatly arranged my altar with a black cloak draped over a small wooden table in honor of them. I have wanted to find peace since they died. But I simply couldn't.

"Santa Muerte, please.... Please help me." My lip trembles. "I know you can hear me." My fingers wrap around my arms as I silently pray, and every single hair on the back of my neck raises.

"You have sent death to follow me." The candle flickers, casting dark shadows that dance across the wall. Sweat beads across my forehead as I lie back down on the sleeping bag. I placed it perfectly in the corner where my bed used to be and ran my fingers through the stray threads of the worn carpet. The only things that scamper across it now were bugs, dust bunnies, and the occasional mouse. At this point, no living thing, not even a rodent, could produce fear in me. Not since the night he came into my life.

"Santa Muerte, protect me, I pray." A long, deep breath escapes with my words until a pounding at the front door rattles the frail frame of the house. The noise pangs through my head and heart, and my body responds with it. I have to leave again.

"Police." A booming voice and flashing lights dance across the window. That first night when they died, the police came and rescued me. This time, they came to take me away. The pounding on the door gave way to heavy footsteps, causing the floor to creak as they drew closer.

"Police, we're coming in!" The voice calls louder this time.

I kiss two fingertips and touch the blood stain on the carpet. "Goodbye, Daddy."

My breath is as light as a feather as I pull my black hoodie over my head to shield my face. One... two... three. I dash out of the bedroom doorway and head for the small washroom in the back where Mom used to work.

"Put your hands up." The voice commands with the sharp sound of a gun cocking.

"Or what?" I turned around to the foreboding light with my palms clear for him to see and look at his cold stare.

"I'm unarmed." Yet another time, Death called to me. But I'm not afraid.

"What's your name?" The officer asks as he lowers his gun. He looks more scared than I do.

"Lucia."

"You again?" He sighs and lowers the flashlight that was beaming in my face.

"What?" I clip back.

"The neighbor called on you again," he says as he eyes my shrine to Santa Muerte in the corner, with the candle still flickering light across the skull. I offer my hands to the officer. He waves his hand back at me instead, gesturing around the house.

"Can I get my rosary before we leave?" I ask as one last request.

"Yeah," he replies.

"My Father had it on him when he passed away...." I turn to the officer with a blank stare. " In this house." I don't want to leave here again, but for some reason, Santa Muerte kept me here, rather than with my parents. Santa Muerte gave me a protector instead. The warmth o Death's wings cover me as I pick up the rosary from beneath the skull and blow out the candle. The rising smoke from the fire that was once there casts an omen on my reality. This life is a vapor. It quickly fades away. Death is my only stable home.

1

FOSTER KID

There is something about being a foster kid that resonates deeply within you. It settled in more when I realized that after my parents died. There was this harsh reality that no one wanted me. Except for him. Death was the only constant in the midst of it all. I can always feel his presence around me, lingering over me. At night, I feel his slight chill down my spine as I lie down to sleep, and His light feathers brush across my back. Something wanted me. Adopted me, even. He was the only one still here. Possibly even the very thing that took my parents.

In this moment, all I felt was warmth across my back as his wings were shielding me again. The gun cocked at me from the police officer was just a painful reminder that only those I love are at odds with Death.

I climb into the back of the police car. The officer rubs his mustache as if in deep thought when He slams the door behind me. This is the lot I got. I huff lightly as I wipe the sweat from my brow and move across the back of the police car. They have me again. My empty stomach churns as the houses I see through the window grow farther away, with each mile away from my real home in Oakcliff.

Miss Rose's weary eyes peer out from behind the door as it opens to the late-night police officer banging on it. She shrugs, and her eyes lack enthusiasm as she sees me next to the officer. Yes, she reported me missing, but she doesn't want me, just like the others.

"Thank you, officer. We will try to make sure this doesn't happen again." the officer nods and she shuts the door. I had become all too familiar with them already.

"You're going to have some tea," she says, walking to the kitchen, "Might help you sleep."

"Sure."

She pulls a tea bag from the cabinet. "So where'd you go, Luce?"

"My parents' house," I swipe my arm across my jacket and let the dirt that had caked on me over the last couple of days slowly shake off. She slams the cabinet shut once she gets the mug out of it. "And why were you there?" an edge to her voice.

"To help me finally sleep... maybe." The truth is that since my parents died, sleep has eluded me. I chase after sleep every night, only to be met with the phantom that fills my nightmares. Each time, he finds me in the most vulnerable place. His deep, penetrating eyes look into mine, and his fingers coil around my neck. The edges of his teeth would meet my veins. I would find myself there, paralyzed in fear. Would he take me too? Just like he did with everyone else? But for some reason, he never does. He kills everyone I love, but his dangerous temper never seems to fall on me. Is it love or hate that inspires his odd and violent behavior? Perhaps he loved me?

"Luce." The mug clanged down on the granite countertop. "When is this going to stop?" I could tell by the annoyance in her voice that she was not bothered by the fact that I wasn't here the last couple of days. But I would choose to sleep next to the blood stains of my father on an old, worn carpet, and inconvenience anyone. It takes as long as I can sleep in peace. The only times the nightmares stopped were at my parents' house.

"I don't know." The truth is, the last couple of days... I finally got some rest. It's like, when I am near my old home..." I pause and glance down at the warm mug in my hands in contrast to the chill I felt from speaking about this. "The house where it all happened is when I can finally rest." I pick up the mug with the tea steaming from the cup. My weary body begins to slink into the chair. I blink slowly. Did she put something else in this? It tasted weird, like a strong herb.

"Go to your room." She says through clenched teeth.

"Alright then." I replied. She nods.

My chest heavy, I drag myself to the room with the rickety wooden door. It's a little better here than my bedroom at my old house, but this, even this, is not my home. I run my fingers through my hair as tangles lightly snatch between my nails. I want to rest, but can I? Will if I'm not close to where they died? I peel off my dirty hoodie from the last couple of days. The rosary from my pocket lands on the carpet beneath me. Would this help, maybe? I rest the rosary on the palm of my hand. It seems to help at least when I pray with it to Santa Muerte. The beads glide over my head and down to rest on my neck and the cross lays against my chest. Maybe this will save me?

"Daddy, I would choose you over this." A chill running down my spine reminded me that Death is here, and he is the only one who wants me now.

The emptiness of the walls around me reminded me that I found myself in this harsh reality. The dining room smelled of old furniture and stale chips. Possibly from the dinner Miss Rose had offered last night. Life had another curse to come upon me today, and she sat at the table, nibbling at the bowl of cereal in front of her. Entranced by her phone, she texts rapidly. Who knows what or who would want to talk to her?

My breath is heavy now as I walk over to the pantry door. Her very presence gnaws at me as she sits at the table texting away. I know she can't stand me either. Mallory is a foster kid just like me. I don't know what her issue is, but my very existence seems to be a threat to her. Her own insecurities translated to detecting anyone else getting attention besides her as condemnable. She coated herself in splotchy self-tanner and bleached hair rebellion. Commodities that were probably stolen from the CVS across the street from our school.

"What's that you got around your neck?" Her high-pitched voice, like nails on a chalkboard, pipe up as I place my bowl at the table. I ignore her and open the fridge to find the milk. There is none.

"You found God finally? Decided to walk away from your weird witchcraft shrine?" She keeps on. I turn to look at her. Her clear blue eyes challenge me like the police officer with the gun had last night. I grit my teeth as I hover around the fridge searching for any bit of milk for my breakfast. I peer at Mallory's glass and then at the empty jug in the trash.

"Can I have some of that milk for my cereal?" I ask.

"No." She takes a sip of the glass. I slam the fridge door shut and sit in the wooden chair cata-corner from her at the lopsided table Miss Rose had in the nook. She stared down at the one thing that made her feel important —her phone. I didn't understand her attraction to it. If she wasn't bothering me, she was scrolling or texting...endlessly. Maybe it was an escape for her from the painful reality she had, or the ability to have power or control of something outside of herself. I can understand that at least.

"So, where were you the last couple of days? And where'd you get that?" Mallory pointed to the rosary on my neck.

"I found it." I broke the silence between us. She didn't need to know its real origin.

"Oh, so it's not yours!" She looked back at me. I pressed my hand against the wood-grain table.

"Of course it is," I bite back. It was my dad's, but I stayed silent, not trusting her with even this tiny truth about myself. I swear, this girl's presence in my life is proof that the night my father was taken from me, God and all his mercy had left me, too.

She snarls at me again before looking back down at her phone. Her nostrils with an irritated nose piercing flared as she sipped on the milk left in her glass. I want to punch this girl in her face. Instead, I take a bite of my dry cereal.

Miss Rose's voice trails down the hallway as she slowly walks into the kitchen.Miss Rose never announced herself, but instead shouted into the void of any room when she talked. "The Case Worker is going to be here soon, Luce." Her voice filled and bounced off each empty wall. I held my spoon tighter as I looked up at her with wide eyes. Fine, I don't want to be here anyway. Mallory smirked at me, holding the milk glass up like she was holding a wine glass with a sparkling merlot.

A light rapping at the front door stopped me from storming away from the table. Miss Rose scampers over to the door and opens it to Emily, a young, fresh-out-of-college social worker. Her short bob haircut, skinny jeans, and blouse gives strong millennial vibes. She's the best caseworker I've had since Rowan died. He honestly didn't compare to any other I had.

Miss Rose waved her arm for the caseworker to come in, and then he walked in behind her. I swiveled in my seat, turning away from the table.

"This is Santiago." Emily offered an introduction. A guy wearing a leather jacket that fits tightly around his waist, cargo pants, black leather boots, and carrying an army-green duffel bag slung over his shoulder. His dark eyes lifted to me and then to Mallory. Her spoon stopped mid-air as she eyed him up and down. She looked at me and then back at him. My heart beating in my chest left me second guessing the reckless choices I made the last couple days. Did I want to leave this home now?

"Miss Rose." My gaze stopped her. "I thought the social worker was coming to take me to another home?" I zeroed in on her aged eyes with slight decline .

"They needed someone to take Santiago in." Her brows furrowed as she didn't seem happy about whatever was happening. I knew her motives. She is only here for the meager paycheck they offered her for each one of us.

"Let me show you to your room." She walked down the hallway. Santiago's mouth turned upwards with a slight smile revealing a dimple on his cheek . *This is going to be interesting.* My lips perk up a little, and I take another bite of my cereal.

" Great, someone else to deal with in this hellhole. But at least he's hot." Mallory broke the silence of the breakfast table.

The rest of the morning passed slowly as I sat on my bed waiting for a moment to meet this new guy ...*Santiago*. I have less reasons to run away now. I may have found someone who I might be interested in. I lingered by my bedroom door as Emily and Miss Rose walked back down the hallway until I finally heard a noise from his room across the hall from mine. *Ok, I'm going to do it. I'm going to introduce myself. It's not every day a guy like him gets to live in the same foster home as me.* I push out into the hall, pleased to find it empty and raise my hand to knock on the new guy's door with the faint sound of Metallica behind it.

"Come in..." A voice inside replied. I pushed open to see Santiago smiled at me standing next to the dresser in the corner. It was worn , with broken knobs and disjointed shelves that he was sticking his clothes neatly into. Santiago lowered the music volume on his phone as I walked in. "Metallica? Nice." I pointed to his phone as he sat it on the nightstand. I eyed his cellphone. How did *he* get something as expensive as that?

"I have taste," he smirks.

I nod in agreement, looking around with eager eyes at his belongings scattered across the bed. His leather jacket that he wore earlier was resting on a desk chair in the room with his combat boots next to them.

"I never got your name." He interjected.

" Lucia, but I go by Luce," I reply, extending my hand to him. He takes it with a grin. Amused by the fact that I would formally give him a handshake.I look into his eyes. They are light brown with shards of gold flecks within them. Enthralling.

"So …Whats your story?" I ask. There is always some story behind why someone has ended up in foster care. Mine was one of the unusual ones. Normally a kid found themselves here by neglectful drug addicted parents, or someone who simply couldn't handle kids. Mine otherwise , died.

"The last family couldn't handle me." He muttered and rested on the bed.

"I know how that goes." I sat down in the chair wearing my leather jacket. The sun beams through the window down on him and accentuates his jawline. His deep brown eyes, soft black hair, and…. light dimpled smile. I don't know if I have a reason to run away from this home anymore.

"What'd you do ?" I prod him. There has to be something behind that innocent look.

"You seem to be familiar with the system. Emily said something about Miss Rose wanting to place you somewhere else. What'd *you* do ?" He questioned back. He stepped forward closer to me. His tall frame looming over me.

My body froze . What the hell? I'll tell him my vices I guess.

"I run away frequently. There isn't a real home for me since my parents died." I replied.

.” His hard eyes softened as if he knew how I felt . Or he had some level of sympathy for me.

"I got too many traffic tickets." He confesses and steps away from me.

"Traffic tickets?"

"Yeah," he nods.

"You drive?" Learning to drive isn't easy for us kids in foster care much less having something to drive. I didn't have the chance to drive on my own or even get a car in this place. With his phone and now vehicle, I wondered how he had access to such funds.

"The bike I own would be kind of dumb if I didn't." He added.

"A bike?"

"A motorcycle," he clarifies as if it shouldn't be a surprise.

"How long have you been in the system, exactly? You come from some money?"

"Since I was eight." He replies matter-of-factly, like he had nothing to hide or be ashamed of.

"And you?"

"Same." My eyes wander over to a Les Paul guitar he has sitting in the corner. I slowly pick it up and study the polished frame on every point of the guitar.

"Where are you getting all this fancy stuff?"

"You really want to know?" He asks.

"Yeah... I do." . Again , I felt like his tall frame overpowered me . I stood still with my eyes staring square back into his . I wouldn't let him intimidate me .

He leans closer to me with a slight smile, "Street races." He replies.

"That explains the tickets." I lower the guitar.

"So ... How long have you been in this home?"

"Too long. But don't change the conversation." I held him with my eyes. "Where do you race?"

"Lockwood and Main."

My hand let go of the guitar neck, slamming against the wall . His eyes flinched. I knew exactly where that was. My old neighborhood right by the cemetery where my parents were buried. Before they died, I would hear the cars or motorcycles ripping through the streets at night. Almost like a symphony that I would fall asleep to at night as a kid. Daddy had a bike too. Each memory I held in fondness with him was tied up with him riding, working on or talking about his bike.

"So you're good at racing?" I turned to Santi, leaving the guitar in its restful position on the wall.

"You can say that. You want to watch me sometime?"

"Sure. I'll see what you're made of." I pulled away from his body, close to mine at this moment. I didn't want to be unphased by the sexy view in front of me. His tight black shirt covered his chest, eye level to me.

"I have a race tomorrow night." He adds. "We can leave when Rose goes to bed." I stare back at him with wicked eyes. I can tell already ... *he is just like me.*

"Okay, *Santiago*." I exaggerate his name.

"I go by Santi."

"Right." I wink at him. "Catch me before the race tomorrow night then."

I walk out of the door, my feet dragging across the carpet, until I find myself in my own room. A humble abode that I believed to be the best place I can be.... at least for now. I turn to my dresser and take off the rosary from my Dad and lay it on the top. I wonder if I could find a place, a home, with these races. The roaring through the streets is what made my heart beat faster. Just like the times I held onto Daddy as he zoomed around our neighborhood streets. I want to feel that free again. The wind blowing through my hair, and every care of the world behind me as I held tightly to him.

I breathe in deep. The wings, the gentle touch I remember since the day that freedom was taken from me, sweep across my shoulders. *Death is here again.*

2

HAUNTING PRESENCE

A flame above the candle swirls and lights the dark void around me. The rosary dangles over the flame, each bead highlighted in the flickering light that dances around it, ready to consume it. This life may be a purgatory for me, like I'm paying for the sins of my father with all this pain. Like this life *is* the all-consuming fire of an eternal hell that my Abuela spoke of.

"Come on, Luce," I tell myself, "You can do this." I continue to dangle the rosary over the fire .If you remove this from your life, he will go.

"Burn it, Luce. You can do this. Death will leave you alone if you do this."

20

My fingers tremble as I let the rosary down over the flame. The silver of the beads begin to light up but I can't. I just can't. I whimper and raise the beads to my chest. The warmth of the flame on my chest like His wings, as the fire is to the rosary. The flames are ready to swallow it whole. But they simply can not go. Death is my eternal reminder of my mortality. He is always there. In the same way, I was dangling above eternity.

But now I am ready for death to consume me just like it did with every person I've loved. My mother, my father.... even with Rowan. That night, the night I'd lost him, I'd held the rosary in my hands as Death consumed yet another soul I loved. He wasn't just anybody; he had been my advocate. Rowan was the only comfort in my life... at least until he was no longer here.

"I love you, Lucia. I'm only here to protect you." Death's voice slithers across me. I knew it. He was going to take me there again... to remind me.

The ground beneath me quakes along with my body as I sit frozen in the city around me. My hazy eyes take in the bustle of the busy streets, rushing bodies, and cars set for unknown destinations whirling around me. The rhythm of the unfamiliar city matches my heartbeat, fast, disorganized, and without reason. Why do I find myself here again?

I am in my twelve-year-old body. I didn't know where to go then and I don't know where I am meant to go now. I had run away that time, from a home that was bad in a different way than the one before it, and now I was frozen on the cold metal bench beneath me as the only thing grounding me in this moment. Warm tears flow from my eyes. A signal that I desperately wanted to be found again. But why did I keep running if I wanted to be found?

Then I see him. His gaze, pulling me to him. My heart calms to a steady rhythmic beat as his feet cross the yellow lined crosswalk. His calm smile immediately soothes the tornado in my soul. I feel his arms pull me into his warm embrace, contrasting the cold of the bench and city streets beneath me. Rowan is here. He came for me. A blurry scene clouded by the tears in my eyes plays before me. His hand extends out to me. "Let's go home." He says gently.

But was home even a place? Maybe it was a feeling, a touch? A gentle reminder that home wasn't found in the foster home I lived in, but in Rowan's warm embrace. His hugs like my Papi used to give. His arms wrapped around me like the wings that embraced me at night. But was this real?

My heart pounds faster as a loud wail escapes my lungs. I reach my hand out to his, and then he is swept away. The bus ripped him from me like paper caught in a breeze. My hand left shaking as, again, Death took someone away from me. The sound of the bus horn fills every bit of my soul. It resonates the ringing in my ears that started the day my parents died. My knees hit the pavement as I see Death take him on his wings. This is my fault. How could I have let this happen? Rowan was just here and now he is gone.

The voice slithers into my ears again. *"I've always been here."*

I slam my hands down this time, to meet the soft sheets and scratchy comforter over me. This haunting presence wasn't always with me.

My body swings up. My breath comes in short, quick gasps with sweat and tears streaming down my cheeks. Nothing moved me as much as this did. Second to my parents, what Rowan did was pure love. A chill runs down my spine again as the metal that clanged against his body swept through my mind. I squeeze my eyes shut against the memory. "It's over," I repeat to myself, "It was a long time ago. It's over. I'm here...I'm not there."

I love you, his voice rings through me. I feel Death's wings as I reach up to touch my neck. He's reminding me again that he is after me. My heart pounds faster as my hand touches my bare neck.

"My rosary?" I gasp. Did I not wear it when I went to sleep? My fingertips frantically search around my nightstand with no sign of it. I throw myself out of bed and stumble over to my dresser. My hands glide across the top and come up empty. No beads. Nothing. Sunlight cracks through the window as I open my eyes to see clearly. It's not here. I tear through my stuff. I know I had it with me when I went to sleep. Shit! Maybe that dream had a little more to it than I thought? I begin to fumble through a large pile of black clothes in the corner of my room, toss the sheets off my bed, and get on my hands and knees to look under the furniture. Nothing.

I crack my bedroom door open to see Santi standing in the hallway by the bathroom. With him there, I just want to shut the door and retreat back to bed. But I'm out of time since my nightmare hadn't had the courtesy to wake me with my alarm. So instead, I walk down the hallway to the bathroom door, to wait beside him. Country music, a wretched singing voice, and steam pour from behind the bathroom door.

"That's Mallory," I roll my eyes. Santi's mouth leaned upwards. His hair is lightly disheveled at the top. Dark brown spikes of his hair lay around his face. I want to brush my hand through it just to see how it feels. God, why is his face so sexy even in the early morning?

The door finally clangs open to Mallory with a towel wrapped around her torso. She shows no class as she pushes through Santi and I to walk down the hallway to her room with the bathroom's steam escaping along with her. I turn to Santi, signaling that he should go since he was here first.

"Ladies first." He gestures in response with his hand towards the bathroom. I smile, but then immediately regret my decision. The scent of cheap vanilla body wash filled the air mixed wretchedly with the stench of her recent shit.

"What the hell, Mallory!" I shout over the country music that follows her to her room. God, why must I be punished with this girl!? I think I am in purgatory, paying for my sins. I squeeze my nose shut, then glance down at the sink with a pus-crusted nose ring by the faucet. Seriously? I gag for a second and then quickly start to brush my hair and wash my face.

I swipe a nearby washcloth across my face to dry it. At least my washcloth hadn't been touched by that demon. Mallory is very particular about only using her own towels. But I guess I will be sharing towels with Santi. I pause with the cloth on my cheeks as blood rushes to my face. The closeness I will have with this new guy might be a little much. How am I going to keep myself contained around him, all the time? He is undoubtedly attractive with his dark eyes. But I wonder more about him, and his... hobbies. I pull myself from my thoughts and lightly line my eyes with the cheap liner I got from the dollar store, replace my pajamas with jeans and a Pantera tee only to open the door to Santi faster. The door groans when I pry it open, stuck from years of too much steam and not enough maintenance. Thankfully, I know I left a better scent for him than Mallory did for me.

"The nose ring isn't mine. It's Mallory's." I brush past him.

"Okay?" His eyebrow raises.

I rush to pack my bag for the day and make my way to the bus stop. Mallory is already there, holding hands with her boyfriend, Conner. Blonde hair, buzzed short, his typical ribbed white tank and khakis, hanging too low around his waist. Occasionally, he wore a dude rag. For whatever reason... I don't know. They whisper in each other's ears as we wait silently by the bus stop until I see another figure heading out of the house. Santi is walking to the stop as well.

"What grade are you in?" I look at him. "I didn't ask you yesterday."

"Eleventh." He replies.

"Me too." I step up the bus steps as the door squeaks open. Red flashing lights from the bus light up Santi's face as he follows with his backpack slung over his shoulder. Even the way he walks is a bit sexy. Mother Mary, help me! I can't get attached. I want to pray that she would guard me from the feelings welling up in me. Nothing ever stays the same, Luce. Everyone fades away.

"Not me," the voice coils in my mind, *"I will never leave you."* Even when I don't feel the presence of his wings on me, his voice is never far.

"I love you, Lucia." Death's voice whispers as it fades from the front of my mind. I may not be alone, but I'm not allowed to get close to anyone else. His presence becomes more threatening when I do. I can not get close to anyone but Death. I need to stay away from Santi. Turns out Death is a jealous lover.

We walk off the bus one by one, like an army of the future genera-
tion, or the future throwaways. Santi had sat in another seat in the
back with his headphones on, perhaps not to be too close,I guess.
I feel a light tapping on my shoulder as I walk toward the school
building and turn around to see Santi's smile.

"Can you help show me around?" he asks pleasantly.

I look him up and down, and then grab at the paper held lightly
in his hand. I guess I'll help the guy out on his first day. Besides,
how can I say no to those eyes?

Immediately, I feel a heavy but familiar weight on my shoulders.
Not a light tapping this time but the pressure heavy pressure just
like the night my parents died. It's like he can read my thoughts.
The pressure reminds me that no matter how cute the guy is, I'm
not allowed to get too close. Ok, Luce, he's here. Don't get too
close.

I scan the paper while dodging the crowd of kids moving past us.
Mallory slides past us with a disgruntled look, and Conner follows

her. Something a little hopeful, but painful pangs in my chest. This will be okay, right? I gave him the paper back.

"You can just follow me, we have all the same classes. Congratulations!" I tease.

"Well, that makes it pretty easy." He replies.

I guess I have someone more than Death following me around at school today.

Each of our classes pass by slowly. At times, Santi gets a desk by me but not every teacher lets him pick his own seat. I spend my day observing him. Most of the time, he sketches in his notebook, rarely looking up. It seems he's a quiet art kid, most often found in the back of class. Despite his sunny disposition, maybe he prefers some level of solitude. I can admire that.

"Or is it just his first day at a new school?" Death's voice reminds me as I feel the heavy weight of wings on my shoulders again. *"Don't relate too much to him, Luce. He's not for you."*

Lunch hour comes up fast especially now that I have a new subject to study. Not the traditional educational subject though. I twist my fingers timidly under the table and see Santi cross the cafeteria as I slide into a seat across Betty. She was always filled with the latest gossip. She has nothing but drama in her life. I mostly tune her out daily. I have plenty of stuff going on in my own head.

I watch Santi get closer to our table and place his lunch tray next to mine and squirm inside for a second. Maybe saying a sarcastic joke about him might deter him away from me? But my heart didn't have it in me.

"Betty. This is Santi. He moved into my home yesterday." I roll my eyes over to her. Her heavily lined eyelids pop open a little as she chokes on the apple juice she's sipping on.

"Hey sexy!" she giggles. I grit my teeth. Of course, as always, she has no tact.

"So you moved in with Lucia?" She prods Santi. Her eyes scan his torso and buff arms as he settles in at the table. He raises his sandwich to his face and nods at her. No words. Just a nod. He may be put off by her straightforwardness. I can't blame him if so.

"Well, don't have too much fun, Luce.' She winks at me. Heat rushes to my face and instead of a sarcastic remark back, I kick her foot under the table with my clunky boot. It definitely got her this time since her Toms don't compare to my combat boots.

Santi silently picks at his plate before suddenly pushing up from his chair. "I'm going to skip the rest of the day. I'm getting my bike back." He's visibly upset as he walks to the trash can, funneling the barely eaten lunch into it. I gulp. Maybe that was too much for him? I hope he doesn't hate me now. Suddenly, I feel a warmth on my back. Death is here, rewarding me like he always does in these moments. I can tell he's satisfied. I turned back to Betty, clanging on her phone with her big nails. She didn't even notice or care that he left. What the heck? I wonder if Santi will still take me to the races tonight?

3

THE ROSARY

The humid air tempts me to take off my leather jacket as I sit melting in the back of the bus. Even if I didn't have the rosary from my Father, I have his jacket to offer me some level of remembrance for him. The Texas fall offered no mercy to those who dress like I do in all black, leather jackets, denim, spikes, and a band T-shirt. The heat here doesn't care about my desire to have a connection with my Father.

I watch each kid slump into their seats in the rows in front of me. Mallory pulls her bag in, walking with Conner by her side. A silver thing around her neck shimmers in the sun shining through the bus windows. I squint. What is that around her neck? Then she shifts her bag on her shoulder and I see it. A rosary, hanging

30

off her neck. She doesn't even acknowledge me, as if she forgot I ride the bus with her daily. She is so dumb. Didn't she know I'd see it? My chest tightens with the tornado of emotions whirling inside me, ready to clash and destroy her. I'm going to beat her the second we get off this bus.

Finally, the squeaky bus doors open when we arrive at our stop. I rush up the aisle and down the bus steps to grab Mallory's shoulder.

"Bitch." I grab onto her shoulder.

"Who do you think you're touching?" Mallory turns around and looks me squarely in the eye. She flips her hair, as if it's healthy enough to deserve to be flipping. Like she's some shampoo model with her fried hair. That's it, I'm going in for it.

"You have my rosary." I move in closer to her, my fist raised, heading for her ugly face. Her nose wrinkles as she ducks away from my punch. I lunge at her, my hands landing on her shoulders and then her neck in an attempt to get my rosary. As my palms wrap around the rosary, I pause, fearful of breaking it. She doesn't miss the opportunity to strike back, her hand whacking at my forehead. And of course she doesn't miss like I had.

"What's your problem?" she demands, her breath wafting into my face as she stands above me. My throat tickles as I gasp for air.

"Shit! Bitch, give me my rosary back!" I yell.

"Kids!" Miss Rose pops out of the front screen door. "Stop it! Stop," She cries, wielding a newspaper in her hand as if she'll whack one of us with it. She didn't dare. She simply waved it in the air. Proceeding with caution, as the big yellow bus was still paused in front of us. Rose waves the bus away with the same newspaper she warned us with.The bus driver must have decided to move on, as the gear squeaked and the bus rolled away. She wouldn't dare with the bus driver still watching, can't risk her foster license and the paychecks we come with.

"Get inside," Miss Rose orders with all the threat the rolled up newspaper promised and walks back through the squeaky screen door.

Mallory, with sweat beading down her forehead, pushes away from me, fumed inside, and marches for the house. I follow, fuming, behind her.

"Sit down." Miss Rose says sternly. We both sit at the table, across from each other. Knowing both of us wanted to reach over and strangle each other.

"I hate that I even have to waste my time talking to you, bitch!" I look her squarely in the eye.

"Hey! chill it, Luce." Rose orders.

Mallory's chin tilts haughtily; she has the look of someone who thinks she knows it all. Oh yes, she knows it all. She knows that the rosary doesn't belong to her. She knows she stole it out of my room.

"Miss Rose..." I plead, "She stole my dad's rosary. One of the last things I have from him." I stare, willing her to believe me. Her expression suggests that she might but isn't willing to side with me so easily.

"What do you have to say, Mallory?" She asks, folding her arms close to her chest.

"Liar!" she accuses, crossing her arms, "I would never want to wear anything from her."

"I had the rosary with me the night I came back from my parents' house," I protested.

Miss Rose looks up and down at Mallory and then at me. "Do you have any proof that she took it, Luce?"

My jaw tightens. Of course I don't. She knows that, and I know it too. The corner of Mallory's mouth tilts upward, a small snarl contorting her cheek.

"No." I lower my head. If only I had worn the rosary that night instead of keeping it in my jacket pocket.

Mallory sits up straighter in triumph, "I think we are done here, Miss." She looks up at Rose.

I clench at the ends of my leather jacket sleeves. Fuming anger as I rise from the chair. I will prove her a liar, if it's the last thing I do. That rosary means everything to me and nothing to her. It's the prayers of my Father. More than that, the spirit of my Father. The very soul of Death is somehow tied to this rosary. If only Mallory would die because she is wearing it. An untimely death would be nice. Just like every person I've fallen in love with. I wish Death would take this bitch from my life, but he only ever steals the people I love, and I can't imagine caring for her at all, much less loving her.

"Mallory. You have a death wish." I whisper.

As if answering my thoughts, I feel the light brush of Death's wings around me and his presence gives me an idea. I know he won't allow me to die; his protection is absolute. So, anything I might do to her, she can't counter in any meaningful way. It's a simple task, antagonize her until she retaliates. I don't wait for her to reply and storm down the hallway to my room. But on the way I see Santi's bedroom door across from mine and my resolve melts away. I am already on Miss Rose's last nerve, if I get in serious trouble again, she'll have me out of here in a heartbeat. I can't risk it. Not now, when staying here might actually be worth it. I want to learn more about Santi, his races, and the world my Dad was a part of.

"I still want her to die," I mumble as I feel that light flutter of Death's wings against my back like laughter, mocking my request, since we both know hate will not move him to action like my love could.

THE GAMBLE

The setting sun turns the sky into hues of blood red and orange as I stare out my bedroom window and time passes impossibly slow as I wait for night to fall. Each second passing like an eternity of its own. Instead of just sitting there I keep busy wondering why I haven't seen or heard from Santi since he left the lunch room. Miss Rose didn't seem concerned that he never found his way home after school. Had he run away too? My heart drops with the thought.

I listen to the faint background noise of Miss Rose settling in to go to bed as the sky through my window settles into the darkness of night. A faint noise, a rumbling, wakes me from my bed. Is that a motorcycle? The light hum of an engine lowers and my heart beat picks up.

"Luce? Are you there?" I hear a faint voice.

"Santi?" I look through the window. I see him standing there with a smile on his face and a helmet in hand.

"I got my bike, if you still want to come?" He asks, his golden brown eyes staring deep into mine through the window.

"Yeah. One second." I turn and grab my black leather jacket from the hook by my door. Santi smiles at me when he sees the leather wrapped around my shoulders. I slowly pry open my window, careful of trying to soften each squeak as I move it up. The cool night air blows across my face as I settle my foot onto the ground beneath me.

"I haven't ridden a motorcycle since my Dad passed away," I warn him.

"Don't worry," he winks, "I got you."

We shuffle through the darkness and around the corner of the house, my hand now in his. I walk over with Santi to the black and silver motorcycle. A small white sticker across the body of the bike displays his tiktok handle *"@ghostboy99"*.

"TikTok?" I tease him, pointing to the sticker.

Santi simply jerks his head to the side and motions for me to get on the bike. I wonder how it will feel now? The last time I touched one of these was with my Dad. I place my hand on the handle bar and the seat is still warm from the last ride. For a second, my fingers glide across the top of the helmet and I feel weak in the knees. I find myself wishing I could run my fingers across Santi's chest and feel the heat of his skin. But now I only feel Death's wings around me, holding me up, then he flutters across my neck as a slight jabbing pain fills my chest.

"Luce." Death's voice reminds me. I reel myself back in. Don't feel this way Luce. I feel a slight tingle down my spine.

"I don't normally have passengers so I only have one helmet," Santi says as he offers it to me, "should fit you okay though."

I push the helmet back at Santi. "It's too constricting," I reply . Besides, only one of us needs to be protected from Death, and it isn't me.

"I can't not let you wear it." He offers again.

"But-" I try to argue before he cuts me off.

"My bike, my rules." He pushes the helmet at me with finality. Why is he like this? So protective. This is something I haven't felt in a long time. I smile weakly as I give in to his demand and hold onto Santi's waist tightly. The sound of the tires grinding against the cement whirls in my mind. Every inch we move forward is like another pound of my heart and another draw to my last breath with the wind blowing through my hair. I smell the deep scent of the leather as I hold onto Santi's jacket. The musky scent is much like the one I remember from when I was riding with my Dad. The faded memory now vibrant in my mind again.

Santi speeds faster down the street and my adrenaline spikes equally. I want to hold tighter onto him as we zoom past the cars. But the fear I feel is superficial, bright but empty. Because even now I feel Death's presence heavy on my back, inching its way down my spine. It was as if he is reminding me that Santi's show of protectiveness is as empty as my fear. That he is still the only one who would ever really protect me, the only one who would always be there for me, and the only one who matters.

The motorcycle slows and comes to a halt as we approach a large abandoned building in the middle of an open field. Its tall metal walls have swarms of people dressed in leather jackets, vests, and boots loitering around it. The sound of engines revving up collected along with the dust in the wind blowing through the field that surrounded us. Santi turns around to me with a smirk. He lightly unbuckled the strap to the helmet under my chin. The light from the building accentuates the dimple on his cheek.

"Safe and sound." He pats the top of my head teasing.

"I wasn't worried." I lift myself up from the back of his bike, Death's wings pressing heavily on my shoulders.

I turn to Santi with a question in my eyes, "By the graveyard?"

"There's an inside joke here, he smirks and points to the nearby graves. "That is every street racer's next stop." Be it irony or fate, I know this graveyard. Of all places he could have taken me, this is where my parents are buried. I feel a chill running up my spine again, like the graves are calling to me.

I shake off the feeling and nod towards the building. "What's in there?"

"Gambling for the races" he replies. "Come. I'll show you." I trail behind him into the dilapidated building. My body tight with the anticipation of what I'll see there.

The smell of alcohol and cigars permeates the humid air. Smoke clouds with red lights hover over each person casting a ghostly ambiance. We walk through the crowd of bikers, grungy looking kids, and older men drinking beers. Where is Santi taking me? He seems to know exactly where he is going amongst the chaos. His hands plop onto a brown polished bar and he swivels into a red cushioned chair. He nods to the lady behind the bar with perfectly done hair and nails, her boobs bigger than her tight shirt and leather vest can contain.

"I want a shot of bourbon." Santi asks. He slams a couple of dollars on the wooden barstand.

"The usual for good luck?" the bartender confirms with a wink as she serves him the shot.

"Yep!" Santi chugs it and gives his head a shake as the burn works down his throat. He stands there for a second, staring into my eyes, and he runs his hand through his hair. An action I'd love to imitate. I want to know exactly how that hair would feel through my fingers, but the lack of alcohol in my system keeps me from trying.

"So who are the bets for?" I question him.

"Me of course." He says with a serious face that quickly turns into a grin. "Some people like to gamble on who will win. "

My eyes hover around the heavy smoke that fills the old barn, taking it all in. "So when do the races start?"

"Thirty minutes, maybe."

I turn to him but my train of thought is tugged away by a familiar face. Dirty blonde hair, messily wrapped around in a bun, crusty nose ring, and shifty blue eyes, squinting over the dice in her hand. Mallory. And she has... my rosary.

"Oh hell no. Mallory!" I holler. I move like there is a magnet pulling us together to take the rosary from her. My rosary. She pauses as the dice rolls out like the dice of my life suspended in fate's hands.

"What are you doing here?" My shout weaves in with her throw of the dice clanging against the cement floor. I snatch the dice up off the floor and stop just shy of throwing them at her face.

"Gambling." She replies without the appropriate concern and tosses my rosary down to join the pile of money, cigarettes and other valuables up for grabs.

"What do you think you're doing with that?" I seethe and swing my arm towards the pile, and a sturdy hand grabs my arm, stopping me from swooping the rosary up. A man with worn hands and cigarette smoke spilling from his mouth faces me.

"Keep it down little lady." He darts his eyes to my body and back up to meet my eyes with an intimidating stare.

"Fuck off." I glare back at him.

"Let me handle this." Santi whispers into the guy's ear and the guy backs off, as if he knew Santi had some unspoken authority in the room. Maybe he was a better racer than I thought? I stand behind Santi, letting him guard me in the conversation. Fully surrendering to the protection I felt with him at this moment. Santi looks Mallory squarely in the eye. She has a tightened fist, prepared for things to come to blows, with little strength she has anyways.

"I'll bet you for it." Santi's deep voice challenged Mallory. A deep level of betrayal coursing through my body as he holds me back and holds my hand from snatching the rosary away from the pile.

A flutter in my stomach brings me back to where I really am. Is this dude standing up for me? My blood stains my cheeks and I hear Death growl in my ear in warning. I can't let myself feel this way.

"I'm going to win the race tonight." Santi continues fixing my attention back on the problem at hand.

"Oh is that right?" Mallory sneers, "We'll see about that." Her arm wraps around Conner's neck and she kisses his cheek. I have myself tensed up and ready to throw hands again if needed. But the weight of what Santi did pulls me away, urging me to sit back and see what happens. She goes on, "My boyfriend, Conner, is racing tonight too."

I look at her face with caked on foundation waving in front of Santi's. I definitely have no competition in our home on who Santi will like.

"Well see." Santi calmly replies, "If I win, I get to keep it." pointing to my rosery, "If Conner wins, you keep the rosary... and this." He adds a wad of cash on top of the pile.

My heart skips another beat. What did he just do? He bet... for me.

"Santi," I reach for him.

"Dont worry, Luce," He plops his helmet on his head and looks at me. "I always win." He says it like a promise. A smile lights my face and my heart as he walks away, brimming with confidence.

What have I gotten myself into? I wonder as I watch him head towards the exit door. His leather jacket is tight around his muscular arms and his 'punk-rocker' torn skinny jeans are snug in all the right places. My eyes trace up and down his retreating form against my will and I feel Death's wings press heavily on my shoulders.

"I love you, Lucia." His voice hisses angrily, *"Don't you forget who loves you."* Still my body, no, my heart, is pulled to follow Santi outside.

The sounds of revving engines and blaring music from the speakers by the dilapidated building pounds through my head. I took my place among the spectators and watch Santi climb up on his bike, adjusting his black, leather, fingerless gloves before placing his hands on the metal handle bars. My heart pounds a bit faster.

What if I could ride with him someday? If only I could? My hands grips the side of my leather jacket as the engines rev up in unison.

A kid with a gun comes forward to the line of motorcycles and bikers on them. Each person with their own array of leather, jeans and even some flare of their own styled vests. I watch the kid raise the gun to the sky as a sharp popping noise breaks through the rest of the noise and then the fleet of bikes whirls away, leaving a cloud of dust for those cheering on the side lines. My heart beat thuds in my chest, in time with the fast paced music blasting from nearby. Santi is gone, like an angel flying away. The faint sounds of the growls from their engines and screech of the rubber meeting the cement fade as the bikes gain distance.

I turn to look at Mallory, carelessly waving her hands and drinking a beer as she talks to her group of friends. She doesn't really give a shit, all that necklace is to her is money... and control. But to me? That rosary means something. My fists tremble next to my pockets as I contain the anger rising up in me. Let Santi handle this, I remind myself.

Whirling engines in the background come and go, and I pace in front of the building. Ten minutes pass and then, like trying to dodge a bullet, the group of people step out of the way of those who are leading the race. I follow the crowd, scanning the cluster of bikes for the one I recognize, I notice him. Santi is coming in first! I watch him sweep over the course like he has angel wings...

or dust, clouding over him. His tires meet the red spray-painted line across the cement, and the crowd roars.

"Fuck yeah!" Every cell in my body melts as Santi pulls his helmet off and nods at me. Those golden brown eyes. I don't linger too long and trot over to Mallory and her group of friends, each one of them squarely staring me down.

"Hand it over." I put my hand out, lacking the patience to wait for Santi to back me up.

"Why should I?" She waves her middle finger in my face. "No."

A thud in my chest calls me to move closer and stare her down more, "Give it over now!" I bark back. A stiff presence holds back my arm from punching her. Fuck, Muerte. Are you seriously siding with her right now?

A shadow forms across the ground, as another familiar presence comes up behind me. Sweat beading across his face, still from the rush of the race. "Hand it over." Santi demands, hand held out. Conner trots up beside Mallory, waving a wad of cash in Santi's face. "Want this?" He prods Santi.

"You can have the money." She grabs the wad from Conner's hand as his eyes widen with disbelief. "But I'm keeping this piece of trash." Her lips pushed out in a pout like she's a little kid back talking.

"You know it's not trash." I hiss. My eyes locked on to her.

"Hey," booms a voice that quiets the growing chatter around us. "What's going on here?" We all recognize it wasn't a question, but a demand for submission. We turn to see a tall, rough looking older man with wrinkles lining his face standing behind us, arms crossed and expression stern.

"She bet that rosary for the race. Santi won..." My voice leapt up in the second of silence. Santi grabbed my hand as I spoke. He squeezed it a little. Maybe he knows this guy better than I do?

The guy's eyes look up and down at me. I know that look. I need to back off and stay quiet. Strangers aren't easily welcomed into this kind of crowd. He isn't going to listen to me until I've proved I belong.

"Break it up now." The man eyes each of us like a teacher breaking up a school yard brawl. The crowd around us dissipates on his order. Mallory grins at me with the rosary still in hand. She lowers it into her pocket. My teeth grind as I grip Santi's hand tighter.

"I promise. I'll get it for you." Santi whispers to me.

My heart pounds faster at his voice. Can I trust him? I didn't know if I wanted to.

"Come on, Santa muerte." I whisper the prayer under my breath. "I'm going to the cemetery." I escape from Santi's grip on my hand. The crowd of people around us had gone back into the metal building. I hear a crunching noise of gravel under foot slowly getting closer behind me.

"Luce." Santi's voice coaxed me back to him and I was met with his soft yet serious brown eyes. "I am going to get that rosary back." He promises. I stare back into those eyes with doubt.

"Where are you going?" He asks, tilting his head in the direction I was walking.

"My parents," I respond bleakly. I turn away from him and walk to the spot that I remember from when I was eight. The moments were seared into my brain as the pallbearers finalized the worst chapter of my life. Their bodies went six feet under and that was the signal that Death had adopted me. I fall to my knees, letting the grass lightly stain my jeans. The anger that had risen within me earlier fades as my hand traces the tombstone, following the 'Ortiz' engraved upon it. I hear Santi's steps in the ground getting closer to where I'm sitting, but I don't want to look.

"I will never leave you." Death's whisper spoke to me along with the grace of his wings on my shoulders.

"My parents are over there." Santi says from behind me. I turn to see him pointing to an angel headstone a couple rows over. "I know how it feels." He lifts my hand into his.

"That rosary was my Father's rosary… he gave it to me before he died." I close my eyes reflecting on where my knees met that night. Blood pooled around my hands and knees as he handed it to me. I had one last kiss with him before he drew his final breath.

"We will get it back." Santi looks at me with determination.

"Why are you so optimistic?" I prod him.

He lightly smiles. A sharp tooth pointing out of the corner of that smile.

"I have to have hope for something." He replies "Want to meet my parents?" He asks, nodding his head toward the angel marked grave.

"Sure." I stand slowly and brush off the bits of gravel and grass stuck to my jeans. He is introducing me to his parents already? This feels fast, I almost smile at my morbid little joke before a sharp pain strikes through my chest. Death's presence is always closer when I am near the graves.

"*Lucia,* he whispers in my ear, *"don't think too much into this. You can't have Santi, but you can protect him. Stay away. It will be better for him, better for you."*

We walked to the angelic grave stone with 'Rodriguez' engraved along the top of it.

"My Dad used to race, too. I know he would have loved to see me do the same." Santi hovers by the stone. As if he can really talk to them again, his eyes look soulfully at the stone. He has so much strength and hope. I can't deny that his hope is appealing, that I want to have it too. If only I could.

We stand together in the silence of the graveyard, set apart from the trouble makers partying it up in the metal building not far off, and take solace in the presence of our parents and the rare company of someone who understands our loss.

"Let's head back before Miss Rose notices we're gone." Santi says suddenly, bringing an end to the moment of peace. He takes my hand and leads us away from the rows of headstones, leaving the graveyard and our parents behind. The bike roars beneath us, too loud and alive for the mood settling over my heart, as he whisks us away to the home we now shared, but not the one I wanted.

5

Death's Dream

The sound of tires meeting the road and wind in my hair echoes into a song as I feel his wings on my back, protecting me. His presence comforts me as I hold tight to the leather jacket, with his strong arms just beneath. The air around us is warm with the Texas heat I know so well. I rest my head on his back with my arms wrapped around him. The pavement grooves flash before me like an old black in white film until blood slithers and pools in the grooves below us. I pull back from the rider I had clung to, my nails still digging into the leather of his jacket. Drawing in a breath, I close my eyes to see flashes of lifeless eyes and broken bodies in my mind, so similar to the moment the rosary had been given to me. My now shaking body clings to the leather jacket, the only bit of safety I have now. Looking up from the bloody pavement I see our surroundings become familiar.

"No. Please," I whisper and pull back from him. I know where and what we are speeding to. The rumble of the engine beneath me softens as we slow down and we park in the driveway. He's brought me home again. The rider's helmet lifts and the sight is so familiar. I know who this is. He turns to me, the empty sockets of his eyes bright, with the flames of hell consuming him and haunting me. This isn't Santi... this is him, Death. His wings begin to stretch out over me and consume me.

"No!" A hollow scream escapes my lungs. I sit up from the cold sheets underneath me. He's here again. I can't rest. I ground myself by pulling them around my body to cover me just like the deep sorrow I feel.

"Fuck." I pound the side of my bed and turn to the vanity mirror across from me. My jet black curls, the ones I know my Dad admired, line my shoulders and frame my weary face. I scrunch them up into a bun on top of my head, unwilling to fight them into submission today. My instinct is to fight back. Let's see what Death has to think about this. I pull on a tight maroon corset shirt. I line my eyes with a deep black shadow and lips with an equally dark stain and walk outside to the street to the bus stop. Santi is already standing there, lighter in hand. He gives it that distinctive flick, to light up the cigarette dangling from his lips. The emerging morning light beams across his flawless skin as he turns to me and drags the cigarette that accentuates his jaw and high cheek bones .

"I didn't know you smoked." I sneak up behind him. "I won it from the race last night. The one thing I could get at least." He shrugs his shoulders.

"You want a light?" He offers.

"No. I'm good." I reply as the bus squeaks to a stop in front of us.

"Wait." I hear Mallory's voice in the distance as Santi and I start up the bus steps.

"Someone stayed out too late." I chime in. Santi heads to the back of the bus as the putrid smell of weed and cigarettes follows behind from a certain almost late someone. The bus driver's eyes glaring in the rear view mirror tells us he can tell who the smell is coming from too. I suppress a smile and snag the seat next to Santi in the back. Mallory sits up closer to the front, thankfully far enough to keep her stench from burning the hair out of our nostrils. Those around her could be gifted with her welcoming presence this morning while we finally escape her.

"So," Santi turns his head towards Mallory at the front. "What should we do?"

"I don't know." I reply softly. I look down at my boots slightly bouncing from the bus's jolts and turns at each street. I feel like this is so much more than just a physical assault. Why of all things would she want my rosary? Unless, her goal really is just to anger and hurt me? I will not let her get away with this.

"I have a spell my Abuela taught me years ago," I reply, and look back at his gaze. His face holds still for a moment, and then his light chuckle clouds the silence. "I'm serious." His face goes rigid again, as he suddenly realizes it wasn't a joke.

"You're darker than I thought." His eyes shift down.

"Yeah, people shouldn't fuck with me."

The sunrise hits our faces as we arrive at the school and the muggy bus empties fast as students try to escape the smelly remnants of Mallory's late-night activities. I smile a bit, as a group of girls covers their faces. One holds her nose and waves her other hand in front of her face as they pass.

Santi trails behind me as we enter the school. Overnight someone has decorated the building with orange, yellow, and purple streamers, sugar skulls, and bright-colored paper flowers lining the halls, in honor of Dias de los Muertes. Normally school spirit isn't my thing but the decorations brighten a little of my sour mood. Day of the dead is my favorite holiday, especially since the loss of my parents, but even before then. Dias de los Muertos is all about remembering family, honoring our ancestors, and wishing them the best in the afterlife. The sour mood bites back with a vengeance at the thought of my parents and my morbid desire to join them again. My hope is that someday I could join them. I pulled my locker open and almost hit Santi with it after shifting the latch to unlock it.

"What the fuck?!? You need to watch it ." I scold Santi with a light smile, realizing he followed me inside the whole way.

He laughs.What is this feeling I am having again? A little light pulled me out from under Death's dark wings.

"Are you going to the Day of the Dead festival this Friday?" He asks, pointing to the bright orange banner plastered on the wall.

"No."

"Me either." he shrugs. I smile up at him and his unexpected reply.

The bell rings signaling us to make our ways to class. I turn away from him and lead the way to our first class, snagging us seats in the back. I decide this time to lightly trace in my notebook. Maybe Death will leave me alone if I leave Santi alone? Mallory waltzes in and takes a seat at the front of the class with her stench and stupid friends. The sight of her reminds me of that spell and I start making a mental list of what I'll need. A candle? Maybe some bones?

Santi's pencil twitches in his fingers as he leans back in his seat. His eyes roll at the stench, and the familiar face joining the class I note a couple other students noticing the smell too. One places their head down on the table, covering their nose with their jacket sleeve. Another, simply scooches away a bit as they flip through their phone.

I scrawl across my notebook. 'Bones and a candle.' That's all I need. I am definitely doing something to her... tonight. I squeeze my pencil as the lecture starts, and Santi flicks a folded note over to my desk. His eyes glance down to the paper, encouragingly. I lift the paper and slowly pull it apart.

'Would you like to go to the graveyard with me on Día de los Muertos to honor our parents?'

A slight flutter in my chest awakens something that I have missed and internally longed for. This is different. Different than what Death has to offer me. I look up at him with a smile and a quick nod and then set to writing out a question of my own.

'Come do the spell with me tonight?'

I flick the note back over at him and no one notices. Yet another benefit to being in the back of class, along with the less likely chance of being called on by the teacher. Santi reads the note and instead of nodding, writes something back. My heart skips a beat, stumbling over anticipation. The words, painted almost like a tattoo in black ink across the stark white paper. A symbol of the darkness that seemed to dominate the light.

'I love your darkness,' he passes back.

My hands shake a bit as I feel Death's wings brush around me like a warning. What am I doing? I know better. But there is something about Santi, something different, something that draws me to him, like the bright white that surrounds the black words etched on the paper.

6

Death's Spell

Mallory licks at her greasy fingers, slick from the fried chicken that Rose brought home for dinner. A few well worded texts and it was easy to convince our guardian that the greasy takeout was her idea. Normally, seeing Mallory eat ruins my appetite. But tonight, the sight has me smiling around my chicken thigh. Not only is the bone-in eight piece bucket saving us from the bland, boxed crap Rose calls her 'cooking' but is a tool for me as well

Santi sits across from me, quietly staring at his dinner plate. I figure to keep from looking at Mallory. She slams her off-brand soda can on the table before standing up to throw away her plate. I follow behind her with my plate shaking in my hand. Maybe if I have her chicken bones the spell will work better? I look up as

Mallory wipes her hands on her already stained jeans and turns down the hallway. I pull a couple of her bones from the trash. As disgusting as the idea of touching her spit feels, this will be worth it.

My room darkens, as I pull the black sheet I picked to be my curtain, loosening the ruffle to the side that was also tied by an also black hair band. The light outside fades and I hold my single black candle next to me. I place it neatly into my small candelabra. This is the only candle I have left here since last halloween, the others all lost with my shrine at my parents house. A slight knock on my bedroom door startles me. He's here. The sound is followed by a flutter traced down my spine. And I know he's here also.

I turn the door knob and feel the weight of his wings on me. Was it a mistake to invite him for the prayer?

Santi's light brown eyes reflect back at me as I open the door, and I decide that even if this was a mistake, it certainly doesn't feel like one.

"You have the light?" I prod at him and let my eyes trace back down to his pants. He nods and flicks up a lighter from his hand and takes a seat on my bed. I pull my hand out at him. "Thank you." I reply as the lighter falls into my palm.

Soon, I am staring into the flame dancing on the black candle on my nightstand. The orange and red hues bring me back to last night and the dream I had. Was my dream an omen? Will Santi get hurt... just like Rowan and my parents?

My heart beats faster as I breathe in an attempt to regain emotional control. The hair on the back of my neck stands up as I feel Death's chilly fingers traveling down my spine.

"*I am always here.*" Death's voice echoes in my head.

"You okay?" Santi's head tilts to the side. As if in confusion as to why I would stare into a flame for so long. I nod.

"Now let's do this," I reply and pull the chicken bones from the wrapped napkin in my hands. "The chicken bones from dinner?" Santi asks, his dimple slightly showing. That only happens when he smiles. Is he smiling because he finds this silly? Or because he's excited to see what I can do?

"We only need something that was alive and now dead. And to set our intentions into the flame." I brace my body towards the flame. "Let you be scattered, Mallory. Like a broken rosary, you have broken my heart, I will scatter your bones just as these." The grip I have on the bones loosens and each bone falls into place. Each one on their own journey with gravity. They scatter across the night stand surrounding the candle. Shadows spread across the surface as the hollows from the bones give light. My breath slows and the flame flickers again. Lowering my eyelids, I give into the serenity around me. Death's grip begins to tighten on my shoulders.

"*Why is that boy here?*" Death's voice angrily shatters me and my intention.

"Don't worry, Death, I'm here." I whisper back .

"What is that?" Santi steps back as I open my eyes to him.

"What is what?"

He jumps back, "Why are your eyes ... completely black?"

I creep back up toward him. "There is someone whom my soul belongs to."

Santi's eyes look full of fear. For the first time I see the small hesitation of Death in him.

"Um... okay." He shifts closer to the door. "A-are you okay, Luce?"

I feel Death's wings upon my shoulders, and can not turn to Santi. I am frozen in place as I stare into the flame.

"I am more than okay." I respond.

"*Yes, Lucia, you are mine.*" Death's whisper trails into my ears.

"I am." I repeat to myself and blow the candle out on my night-stand .

"I am going to go now. Good night Luce. " Santi slowly walks over to the door, closing it behind him. Did he feel the shift in me? The one when I am united with Death? Those moments are when I feel closest to my parents. As death comes close enough to even enter me. Now maybe Santi will have a healthy fear of him. And not just any fear, the fear that I hold onto. It's the fear that protected me all this time. It was the fear of what I was becoming. The fear of my lover... Death.

7

Date with Death

This morning I had hoped to see Mallory choke on her rice crispy cereal. But instead she endlessly scrolls on her phone with breath in her lungs. 'Some things take time, Luce.' I remind myself that fate has control of this now. I breathe in deep and pour the orange juice into an empty glass from the pantry.

"Santi isn't here." She breaks the silence with her high-pitched tone.

"I noticed." I take a swig of the juice. It's slightly sour, possibly expired.

"Of course you did. And don't think I haven't noticed what he did for you the other day at the race." I place the glass on the counter, and it clangs on the cabinet harder than I imagined it would.

"Lovely morning already, huh?" Miss Rose walks in with squinty eyes at Mallory and me. I feel the stare down from her, trying to break up a fight about to happen. So instead of talking back, I pour the sour orange juice into the sink and walk to grab my backpack for school.

In the still dark morning, the bus has yet to arrive so I'm left waiting in the slight chill of late October in Texas. I pause by the doorway as I notice that Santi's motorcycle isn't parked beside the house. Where did he go? A small shiver goes down my spine as the wings brush against me. Those are the wings that protected me. What happened last night... did that cause Santi to feel scared of me?

"That's it. I'm done playing games with you, Death." I whisper and I hear the front screen door opening behind me.

"Talking to the voices again?" Mallory with her messy bun turns from me and heads to the bus stop.

"Give me my fucking rosary." I demand.

"Get the fuck out of my face, bitch."

I pull my backpack strap closer to my chest. "Let's gamble for it."

"What?" She pauses and turns from walking to the bus stop.

"You heard me. Let's play a game. I want my rosary back. Winner gets to keep it." Death presses against my back, now with the slight tingle of brushing a feather across my cheek. Is Death responding to my demand to stop playing games or my desire to have my rosary back? Does he know it has nothing to do with him, or does he know it's for my Dad?

"It's already mine." Her eyes twinkle along with a smirk that crosses her face.

"What, you don't think you can win in a gamble against me?" I play into her ego.

"As if. Whatever the bet, I'll crush you." She nods, folding her arms over her chest and staring cold and hard .

"Russian roulette." I challenge, "This Friday." I hold my face still to keep the smirk of my lips. I am not afraid of death. I know him. He will always protect me. There is only one person who could die in this gamble.

"You're crazy." Mallory eyes me up and down.

"I'm not afraid." A light brushing of his wings on both of my arms reminds me who I am really playing with. Mallory's eyes shift to the ground with hesitation. She swallows and looks up to the bus coming around the neighborhood corner.

"Deal. I'll get Conner's gun." She turns and walks away as the yellow bus's wheels screech in front of the stop.I stare into the red flashing lights of the bus hitting the pavement. What have I done? Death's wings rest on my shoulders with warmth as I walk up on the bus steps. I sat on the bus with my heart pounding. Maybe I

scared Santi with my spell last night too? What is happening to me
?

"You're closer to me now." The slight tingle of his presence wraps around my body. I swallow hard and lean in on the warmth his wings provide. He truly is the only one who is always here with me.

Death carried me throughout the day with his wings around my shoulders. A warm presence to remind me that he isn't leaving. It seemed so much that time flew by as if he did carry me on them. Once the last bell of the school day rang I saw Santi's motorcycle was parked by the side of the school. I walk to it and lightly touch the soft leather seat. This is another way I could fly. Just like with Daddy. I shake off the ache of my heart for an equally troubling thought, would Santi even want me to ride with him again? What does he think of me now? The fact I've barely seen him today despite the fact we have the same schedule suggests my spectator and I have already scared him off.

"Did you still want to meet at the graveyard on Friday?" His soft voice inquires from behind me. I jolt slightly at his sudden appearance, here I was touching his bike like some creep. I want to ignore his lingering presence behind me but can't.

"I have a date." I finally reply.

"Really?" He walks around in front of his motorcycle and consequently in front of me. A light smirk on his face as he stands, beaming at me.

"Yeah." I nod. Remember Luce this is for him. I must protect Santi at least.

"Want a ride home?" That lightness of his is drawn out by the sunlight as he smiles at me. He looks deep into my eyes. "Not black anymore?" He whispers, scanning my face quickly. I knew it. I knew he could see it too. I was in a partnership with death. Or so I thought. Maybe Abuela can help me?

"Actually, can you take me somewhere else?" I step closer, not shifting my eyes from his.

"Sure." He shakes his head, pulling him from his thoughts. "Where do you need to go?"

"My Aubella."

In tune with my heart beat, I feel the flutter of death's wings again. He is pressing hard this time. I sit on the leather seat, admiring it. The engine vibrating underneath us causing my whole body to tingle as we zoom off the school property. The wind tousles through my air and I hold tight onto Santi's back, arms wrapped around his waist. His stomach is like a chiseled stone, something stable and constant I can hold onto. Constant, steady in the midst of danger. The warmth of his back against my chest is causing my heart to beat faster. I could get used to this.

It's like I am flying, and of course Death Is here as always. He never leaves. Here I am, feeling like I'm flying again but not with Death, not disconnected from life like I was earlier today. I hear the constant beat of Santi's heart as my head presses against his back. Maybe I can finally feel the stability of life again?

I pull off his helmet once he stopped the bike in front of the old trailer home. The once white metal panels that held it up are now worn with cracks and dirt that caked along the side. Weeds grown along the side, and the wooden steps that I remember going up with my Dad were rotting. I step off the bike and shuffle to the side.

"I'll be right back." I nod at Santi.

The wooden steps leading up to the home creak with the pressure of my boots.

"Abuela?" I hear a t.v. humming from inside and I tap on the door and it creaks open. Smoke hovering in swirls, revealed through the sheets she uses for curtains in the windows. A silver reflection of her wheel chair turning appears as she turns herself to the sunlight. "It's me, Luce." I call as I step inside. Everything is just how I remember. Tobacco stained pictures hang on dusty walls above mostly unused furniture, random medical supplies stashed on every surface. The floor is littered with odd bits of trash and objects abandoned where they'd fallen. In the kitchen area there is an ever present stack of empty TV dinner boxes leaning against the microwave and wrapped around everything and already seeping into my lungs is a heavy scent of old carpets, cigarette smoke and menthol. Abuela sits in her wheel chair, facing the TV with the same faded pink cardigan over her shoulders she's worn since I was small.

She winces beneath her light framed glasses. A faded pink sweater hangs over her slight shoulders.

"Abuela?" My heavy combat boots drag across the carpet. A stack of empty tv dinner boxes lean like a tower piled up on a dusty old tv dinner stand.

"Lucia?" her eyes squinted up at me. She pressed the glasses on her nose up.

"It's me."

"Lucia." She caresses my cheek as I sit down on the footstool next to her wheel chair. She clicks off the TV with a shaking hand. Her smile is shining with the little bit of life left in her. Ever since Papi died, she'd slipped from reality more and more. She's capable enough to get around, feed herself, and stay within the frame of her trailer home. But that's it and I fear the day those simple tasks become too much. I look around at the dusty monuments of saints that decorate her home.

"What are you doing here Luce?" She questions and pulls her pink cardigan over her shoulders more. The wrinkles on her face tightening with her faint expressions.

I place my hand on her shoulder. "I want to pray to Santa Meuerte... with you."

She nods in agreement. "You know that Muerte has watched over you since you were a little girl. I have prayed for justice for Gabriel... and nothing came from it."

"I know, I know." I rush her, "But Abuela, there is something else." I clench the edge of the sleeves of my leather jacket. Abuela lifts a frail hand to trace the jacket sleeve. She knows it was her sons. She remembers him more than most other things. "There has been a presence with me since that night." I finally whisper the secret that haunts me if anyone could believe me, could understand, it will be her. Aubella nods and pushes herself to a table tucked into the corner, frail, old hands oddly steady as she strikes a match and lights the single candle that sits there. It's a half melted, white votive encircled by stained glass. The figure of the Grim Reaper drawn upon it. I remember this candle. It was in my dreams.

"Ab..."

She hushes me. "I used this candle when your father died." meeting my eyes, "Let me say the sacred prayer." I lower my head in reverence. Abuelita prays in a hollow tone. "Beloved Santa Muerte, keeper of life and life's mysteries." She reaches for my hand.

"Protector of those who call upon you, we come to you with respect and an open heart." Her fingers began to tremble in the light of the flame. A tear streaks down the side of her weary face as she turns her soulful gaze up at a framed picture of her son, my father, Gabriel, wearing a leather jacket, the one that now surrounds my shoulders. A helmet is held by his waist and his other arm is around my mom. His black harley propped behind the both of them. They were so young in this picture.

"If only Santa Muerte could really bring my son back."

"Abuelita?" I squeeze her hand. I knew her pain too well.

"Mija," she struggles to say. "My dear, Luce." Her cloudy eyes gaze at the spot just above my shoulders, where I feel Death's wings press against me like she knows he's here, like she could see him standing behind me.

"I prayed the night of their death that Santa Muerte would protect you and she did ."She whispers. " she sent Death to be your protector." My breath shortens as I feel his wings across my chest. I look up at the picture again.

"Papi?" I look at his face, watch as it turns into a burning skull. That skull with the menacing fire eyes and wide grin that haunts my dreams and stalks my steps, that knows me and owns me keeps me safe under his crushing presence floated away from me. A distant sound of breaking glass pulls me back and I blink at the bokeh frame where it has fallen to the floor.

"What was that, Lucia?" Abuela looks up at me with innocent yet aged eyes.

"Nothing, Abuela." My hands are shaking, floating lightly above the frame. I sweep up the broken shards on the ground and look at Gabriel, my father. "Can I have this? I gotta to go." I kiss her cheek and step out of the dark swirling room of my Abuela's trailer home and into the glaring light outside.

"Are you all good?" Santi asks. His face hauntingly familiar to the photo of my younger father inside. I blink and rub my eyes. It's not the skull. It's Santi.

"I'm good." But now, it feels like someone else is here too, not just Death. "Take me home please,"

Santi turns around to me as I mount his bike behind him. His light smile beaming at me, just as my father's did in the picture. Was this connected to my father? The sunlight reflects in his smile as he revs the engine to life.

I shift and press my arms around his chest. My forearms caressing the leather and a musky scent of cedarwood and balm inter my breath.

"*I'm the only one you can do that with.*" Death whispers into my ear. I feel the tug of his wings pulling me back. I grasp harder onto Santi's leather jacket.

"When is your next race?" I shout into Santi's ear.

"Day of the dead." He mutters back. My heart drops and I lean closer into Santi. Maybe? Just maybe this could heal me? There would be justice for my Father, by love for his daughter. A promise for a new life before her. Was this what my Papi would want for me? I slink down in the motorcycle seat as Santi pulls into the driveway at Miss Rose's house. But I can't. I can't be with him. I have a date with Death.

8

DAY OF THE DEAD

The rest of the week flew by just like Santi does with his motorcycle.

I sat by the bedroom window, hearing him rev up the engine as he sped away. He must be going to celebrate Day of the Dead. I almost regret not going with Santi but I know what I need to do to keep him safe. A gentle caress of Death's wings glides across my shoulder.

"It's okay Death, I remember. I am yours." I appease his dark interest.

"*I love you.*" Death whispers.

"I love you too. I will be all yours soon."

I think tonight, only one of two things will happen. Either I would shoot myself in the forehead, and Death could finally have me, or even better, Mallory would die of her own stupidity.

"Ready?" I hear Mallory ask from my door way as she cocks the gun in her hands.

"Ready." I respond with a straight face.

Her bleached, frail hair whisks around her face, matched by the snarky personality. Her nose ring flares just as her nostrils does.

"Want a chance at death?" She points the barrel of her boyfriend's gun towards me and plops the rosary on my pillow.

My rosary.

I take the gun from her hands, feeling the weight of it and the cold bite of the metal. "I'm not afraid." I reply, staring back into her eyes. Life is so fragile. It's like a gamble between here and eternity. She smirks as if she's caught me in a trap. If only she knew Death was basically my boyfriend. I hold the cold steel in my hand, slightly shaking. "You loaded it right?"

"Of course, I did," her nostrils flare with annoyance.

I nod my head up, my finger coaxing the cold trigger. 'I'm ready for you. Take me now, just don't take Santi. Please.' I silently pray as I place the gun to my temple. A slight trickle of sweat goes down and meets my chin. I swallow thickly. "You can have me." I whisper. My finger pulls on the trigger. For the first time, I see the white's in Mallory's eyes as she widens them enough for me to see past her false lashes. The sound of an empty click fills the room.

I stare Mallory down. "Your turn." I shove the gun back across at her. Her fingers tremble as they wrap around the handle.

"Your fucking crazy." She squawks back and she throws the gun onto my pillow... next to my rosary.

"That's what I thought." I yell out as she rushes down the hall.

I take a breath to slow my racing heart, crossing the room to take my rosary back into my hands. I hold it tight, overcome with relief, and pull the beads over my head to rest on my neck, where it belongs. Why must Death torment me so much that I can only find peace with this thing? What is the point? I wonder as my shoulders droop with exhaustion. Santi is already gone, Death can have me now. The gun sitting on my pillow calls to me, promising the rest that I so desire. I lift it up and hold the quivering barrel to my head.

"You can do this Lucia Grace. Dad, I am ready to see you on the other side." I close my eyes. There is only one thing I can do. I can only give myself to Death. But can I? Can I take this leap? Knowing about the wings that protect and hold me. He always held me. He always protected me. I knew he wouldn't abandon me tonight. What's the point of life anyways? Death obviously wants me just like he wanted my parents. I don't want to continue this gamble called life. I might as well give in to the wings that hold me so closely. I can finally give into the darkness that caresses me at night. The very pulse within my veins is the only thing that separates us. I could be his eternally .

"I am coming for you." He appears beside me, the dark swirling oblivion that haunts me.

I put my finger on the trigger. A loud clang shakes the house. The rosary didn't protect me. Every sensation around me intensifies. I see the blood pooling around my knees. Then I'm not there. I never was. I've always been here. I blink away the blood as I see the doorknob turning. A skeleton face flashing through my view. A black and white hollow painted figure before me. But his eyes, they are not made of fire. They are brown, warm, and full of life. Santi?

He leaps towards me with the gun in my hand and finger in the pry. "Luce. What the fuck? What are you doing?" He pulls the barrel up and my finger lets the trigger loose. A clicking sound for an empty barrel causes Death's wings around me to evaporate. Instead of Death's flaming eyes, dark brown eyes pierce deep into mine.

"Santi." I latch onto him. My hands wrap around his jacket.

"What are you doing!?" He pulls me back from our embrace and lightly shakes my shoulders. Even with his face painted, I can see his tender lips pressed into a tight line, his head tilted in confusion.

"I…" Could I tell him? My heart pounds faster at the thought of telling him about Death. Surely, that would get him killed. I let my grasp on the gun go. "I don't know."

"Why would you do this?" He asks after a rough exhale.

"I... want to be with my parents," I respond with a blank stare. Santi moves toward me and the street light shining through the window lights his face, bringing every contour of his face into view.

"Your eyes..." Santi lifts his hand up to my cheek, as he darts his eyes back and forth examining mine.

"There is something dark within me." I lean in to him to match his serious eyes.

He lifts my chin to meet his eyes, "I see so much more." He pushes back at my resistance. "I see a girl that wears her scars with pride." He wipes the tears from my face. "You are worthy to your Father." his hand moves up to my temple. "I see a girl shrouded in fears from the past." He pulls an eyeliner pencil from his jean pocket and holds it lightly up to my face. "Close your eyes." The sharp pencil glides across my closed eyes as I breathe out. "I see a girl who wants to mask her pain." He glides the pencil down to my cheek and back up, drawing a line across to my temple. "I see a girl who has survived so much." The pencil meets my lips. The sharp edge traces along my cupid's bow. Then he crosses past my lips light enough to add a smile. "And still smiles everyday." He pulls the pencil up and down, drawing stitches across the edges of my mouth. I feel his soft breath on my neck. "Open your eyes." He whispers. I lean back looking at the mirror across me. I lift my eyes to see that he had drawn the traditional Day of the Dead mask on my face, just like his. "Do you want to go to the graveyard with me?" His hand traces across my temple and brushes my jet black hair from my face. His eyes match mine. His breath matches mine. In this moment, I simply could not escape his tender gaze. "It is not death that is your destiny Lucia, its life." My heart is beating again as the words he says fills my soul.

The screechy screen door opens as Santi takes me away from the prison that Death held me in. An entrapment that I have lived in since the day he took my parents. Santi hovers over the motorcycle for a second before mounting his bike. Sweat traces his neck and chest lightly glimmering in the moonlight. 'Mary, help me!' I pray and grasp the beaded rosary around my neck.

"Ready to go?" He extends his hand toward me.

A cloud of dirt trails behind us as we speed to the graveyard. My foot falls into the deep grooves of pressed gravel left by Santi's tires as I hop off the back. Santi offers his hand to me after getting off his bike, his touch magnetic as my hand clasps into his. Electricity waves through my veins. Death is here. "Come with me." Santi whispers to me as the crowd of celebrators, honoring their loved ones, become simple figures in my peripheral view. His eyes draw me in.

We walk toward dusk and the trail that leads to the tombstones. The sky's hues match the beautiful pink, yellow, and red marigolds strewn across the graveyard. A perfect combination of colors for a festival such as Dias De los Muertes.

The path is lit up by the array of candles and monuments that people have decorated each grave stone with. Almost like a beautiful painting every person's individual pain of who they have lost. Candles sit like orbs floating around each headstone we pass. Santi's hand intertwined in mine as our boots crunch against the graveyard's fallen leaves. Marigold petals are scattered across every stone. Music fills the air, but even more, the faces of skulls, painted like ours, to represent that all of us are immortal.

Death's wings press on my shoulders. "You're here, aren't you?"

"What?" Santi asks gently.

"Oh, I was praying." I brush off my comment as the wings press harder on my shoulders. "Where are we going?" I squeeze Santi's hand. I'm not leaving him this time. Maybe I have a chance at life.

"My parents." He replies as we walk up to a single stone. 'Rodriguez.' is etched into the stone. Candles are lit beside the grave, dancing in the light wind blowing through.

"I put these here earlier." He remarks. "And..." He pulls my hand to follow him and as we walk past the rows of graves, I know exactly where we are going. A soft white lace blanket laid in front of it. Marigolds, candles lit on each side of the stone and a small basket. "And for your parents." He picks up a bunch of bright yellow marigolds lying by the stone and offers them to me. My fingers tremble, as I feel the sharp pang from Death, demanding my attention. I am still his as I reach for the bunch of flowers. The orange-gold petals lightly sprinkle onto the dirt that hides my parents underneath, and I turn to Santi with a slight tear down my cheek.I turn to him in solace, and he wipes the back of his hand across my cheek to save the make up drawn across my face. My head lands on his shoulder, and immediately, a pain goes through my chest. In an attempt to rest my body, I breathe in deeply. The sharp pains are still there. 'Death is mad at me. I raise my head from his shoulder. 'I can't be here with him.' Small thorns lightly pierce the palms of my hands as I hold onto the flowers tightly. I lower them onto the grave.

"Why did you do this?" I ask. 'If only I could stay here longer.' Besides, I didn't want him here with me. Not Santi, but the wings. The one that had never left me alone since that day.

"Because you're worthy." Santi picks up a small candle by the headstone. Did he prepare this for me? For my parents? He picked up a small table cloth behind the stone. My breath stills for a moment. He flickered a light and rose it to the candle, then offers it to me. I look up at Santi's eyes. The smoothness of his brown eyes are highlighted in the candle's flame.The slight glimmer of his eyes was enough for me to surrender every fear of death coming after me.

"For my parents," he raises the candle toward his parents grave. "For your parents." I smile slightly. He holds the candle close to himself. He pulls out from behind him some little chocolate dipped strawberries with Day of the Dead faces painted on them. "And for you." I giggle as he raises a strawberry to my mouth.

Another tear trails down my cheek, lightly carrying my makeup away. Is this love? I look at the gravestone that is all that is left of my Mother and Father. They were both whisked away by my lover, Death. I miss them, but the reality is that Death is always here. For all of us. Not even the immortality of young love can escape his grip. Each moment we rise and breath we take in is just one step closer to him. Even if we aren't taken away in youth, our bodies mold to his dance. The pursuit of Death never ends.

"What's on your mind?" Santi interrupts my thoughts. I turn to his light eyes.

"We are all in a romance with Death," I reply.

"But life comes first." He places a light thumb on my cheek and leans in to kiss me as the moonlight shines upon us. I feel his breath heavy on my neck and I press my hand onto his hard chest and feel his heart beating. Is this how life feels? Our lips collide into a symphony as he pulls his body closer to mine. Is this love? Blood rushes to my face. The moonlight casts shadows on his chest as he pulls his shirt off and embraces me. I lift my shirt off in turn and lean back on the lace tablecloth. The ground underneath me, but this time, I don't feel that Death is going to swallow me whole into a grave. Santi's body instead consumes me. For the first time in years, my body fills with life.

9

GORGEOUS NIGHTMARE

Death's cold, bony hand traces along my cheek. No life, just a skeletal head turns to look at me with flames in his eyes. Black feathers fall from his large wings that sit above his leather motorcycle jacket on his back. Each time he moves them closer to me the flame around his head flickers, until his wings are over my shoulders and I am wrapped in his warmth.

"My Lucia, you are such a gorgeous nightmare." His eyes with flames flicker before me.

"I'm not going anywhere." He whispers *"I'm here, with my love for you, for eternity. You are mine."* Despite his fiery presence, I am held here, frozen in time. Every bit of darkness spilled from my

80

inner being. Is this love? I cherish the darkness of his wings that he wraps me with. But is this love?

My breath shortens as I feel the sudden cold cement of the cemetery's gazebo floor. Santi's warm leather jacket above me contrasts the cold with warmth and comfort just as Death's wings did. I trace my hand on Santi's chest. It slightly moves under my fingers. I want to believe that I am dead, that I no longer could feel this sensation of cold or warmth, and that Death had taken me in my dream. After last night, I know I provoked him. The fear that paralyzed me suddenly shifts to an overwhelming peace. Death hasn't taken Santi.

What is it about him that causes this absolute calm to come over me? It's like I have been followed by a sense of tragedy and death since I was eight. I am always waiting for the next ball to drop, the next tragedy to settle in and hit me once more. Death always reminds me that I only belong to him. But then, Santi. He's so perfect. I turn to him laying next to me on the cold, hard pavement, his body and arms completely folded over me. I watch the rise and fall of his chest as he breathes, see the pink of his cheeks and flutter of his eyes as he sleeps. This isn't just a moment of admiration, but a moment of healing. I gently caress Santi's arm. This is what I have been promised. Life.

I must admit that I no longer only feel connected to Death, but to Santi too. The warmth of each arm embracing me, holding me safe kept me sane in this moment. I don't want to die. Not like my parents did. But what if this means that I can't escape Death like they did?

I peer at him and the rows of graves around us. Ever since he came into my life, I've tasted peace. This calm that could transcend the presence of Death around me. An absolute knowing that there can be life around me. The vivid colors of the trees and flowers blooming around me. That they are not just calling for my brutal end. At his side, I have hope to live again.

A small trigger of Santi shuffling pulled me from him. He slightly raised his body up and it removed the soft leather jacket from my chest, and his. He has the slightest, sweetest grin that caused the chill in my spine to dissipate.

"Did you sleep well?" He asks, his voice soothing the very edges of my soul. It feels like a sweet honey that coats the rawness of me and brings a soothing to the sting of death.

"I... did." I lift my body up and raise my hand to clasp my forehead.

We both gathered up all the things that had made last night the most magical evening for me. The candles we lit were all now blown away. The graveyard was covered with flowers. Orange, gold, blue, and red hues trailed along each grave, painting the life that was breathed back into every soul by their relatives and loved ones last night. I reach out to touch Santi's hand as we walked to his motorcycle. The warmth of his hand reminds me, for the first time in a long time, of a feeling of relief. As we pass my parents' grave on the trail and then Santi's, I see the names scrawled across the stones. This is what they would want for us. This is what my Papi would want for me.

Santi straddles the motorcycle and hands me his helmet. As pure chivalrous fashion would call him to do. I know I don't need it, but I take him up on his offer. What if Death is out to get me more now? A slight thud in my chest reminds me of the bitter truth that tragedy could strike at any moment and end this beautiful scene.

The police car in front of the house was undeniable. Great. Another run in with the cops.

"I have no idea where they went, officer." I hear Mallory's squealy voice inside the house. My heart pounds harder as I pull the screen door open.

The officer turns around and levels an appraising glare at Santi and me. Both of us have smeared Day of the Dead makeup across our sweaty, worn faces and look like the rumpled messes sleeping outside left us as. He rolls his eyes. "Looks like you may have your answer."

"We were celebrating our dead parents last night. For Day of the Dead. It's pertinent to our culture." I chime in to deescalate any consequence Rose may have for us. Who could punish two orphans for remembering and celebrating their dead parents?

"Culture is important, but so is respecting authority," the officer scolds, "And neither of you had permission to be out all night."

I grit my teeth and nod my head in the closest to an apology I can manage.

Satisfied, he turns his attention back to our guardian, "Mrs. Rose." The officer leans toward her. "You can have your ability to foster in question if you keep having situations like this."

I see the fire in her eyes as the officer turns around and walks out without even letting her respond.

"Go take a shower." She turns to me and Santi. "Get that smoke smell off your clothes." She yells down the hallway when we leave to do as we've been told.

Santi and I walk down the hall with Mrs. Rose fixated on the front screen door. My heart skips a beat as Santi opens the bathroom door at the end of the hallway. His charming face peers from behind the bathroom door once he walks in confidently. He winks at me, nodding his head for me to come inside.

The adrenaline hits my veins, and I chuckle a little as he closes the door behind me when I rush in. He locks the door, a small metal sound that signals. I'm his now. Santi's lips meet mine, mashing together like we find our very sustenance in each other.

Mrs. Rose pounds on the door interrupting our kiss. "I know what you're doing. You'd better not get pregnant." She scolds.

I laugh. "We're just taking a shower... like you said to do."

The water drips down my body, washing away every bit of sweat, tears, and makeup from yesterday. Every magical thing from last night is held in his embrace. His hands trace my body, remembering every sensation from last night. His arms around me like forces of life pouring into me, giving me the will to live another day. I turn to Santi to kiss him again, and a stabbing pain glides down my spine and I have to wonder, will Death allow this?

10

DEATH'S RACE

Santi's hands caressing my body are replaced by a towel as we sneak off into our bedrooms. The cool of the air chills my heated skin. My heart skips a beat as I shut the door, pull my towel past my hair and put on new clothes. My phone beeps with 'Santi' written across the screen. Accepting the call, "What do you want, now?" I answer, giggling.

"Want to go to a race with me tonight?" His tender voice coaxing my body and soul again.

"You bet."

"Of course." He replies and then hangs up the phone.

A tightness around my throat causes me to pause.

"You. Are. Mine." Death's voice hisses in my ear. A tear rolls down my cheek. His hand is clenched around my neck. I must submit. I can't forget this.

"I'm sorry," I whisper into the void of my room to placate my haunting specter, "I'm yours." The words ring more true than I had meant them. There is something about this voice that has always followed me. Since the day that my dad died. It haunts me, always romancing me, giving me a reason to live or to die. I had been so finished with him just hours ago, but there is still something pulling me towards the lover I've always known. I haven't felt as alive in ages as I did with Santi but Death has always been with me, always loved me when no one else could. How could I have betrayed him like that? "I'm sorry," I whisper again with more conviction this time, "I love you. I've always loved you." I tell him, but get no answer.

His silence stings as I get ready for bed and snuggle down in between my scratchy, thread bare sheets. Death has always been closest to me at night when I sleep, and even though it's only just past dawn, I feel him settle down alongside me in the bed. His presence is so familiar and the tingle down my spine feels like the beginning of forgiveness. Will he be there in my dreams? Waiting for me? What sort of nightmare will I face as punishment for my indiscretion with Santi? The thought fills me with spikes of fear but I know whatever punishment I receive will be deserved though that doesn't make them any easier to face.

Death's touch is cold and I shift under my blankets to find some kind of warmth and comfort. But there is none to be found. I'm left tossing and turning despite the exhausting pulling at me as sleepless hours roll by. Fear and guilt tie my stomach into knots, and my bed starts to feel like it's only made from lumps and protruding metal springs. My treacherous thoughts turn to the leaves and concrete I slept on the night before and how much more comfortable I had been wrapped in Santi's arms and I give up on the idea of restful sleep entirely.

I raise my lighter's fire up to the cigarette held tightly between my lips, needing the hit of nicotine after so many sleepless hours. The light igniting not only the remembrance of my parents and the violent death they had, but the passion still within me for their justice. I want this flame to ignite within me and give me the will to live longer. But still, Death's presence lingers around me.

I stand on the crumbling dirt under my combat boots as a gang of other racers pull around, scattering gravel clouds around us. I spot Santi in the back of the line and pull a drag on my cigarette. I turn around to see Mallory on Conner's bike. She's straddled his waist with a scanty skirt, leaning into his body. Just let me barf in my mouth now.

"You're smoking now?" Santi asks. I shrug and take a drag of my cigarette. The flicker in his smile looks just like my dad's in my Abluela's picture frame. The stars in the sky behind him like glowing orbs. He has a ghostly familiar presence to him.

"Watch me smoke this race, Luce." Santi straddles his bike. He turns the ignition, and the bike rumbles to life underneath him. In unison, each rider follows, like a symphony of roaring coming from each vehicle. The sound calls me to defy what I have always known, that I belong to Death. But what if I don't want to? What if I am tired of being silent and alone, with one foot chained to a grave and a master who allows me no one else? What if I want to be free? Be free to rumble and roar and run, with as much life as these bikes, coiled with speed and the itch to race. What if I let go of fear and Death?

I put my hand on Santi's handlebars. "Can I race with you?" I ask, fast and out of breath.

Santiago smiles, holding out his hand out to me, and I take it. "Sure. You can ride with me, Luce."

I jump on behind him, clasping my arms around his leather jacket. 'Sorry Death,' I silently pray, 'but I don't need you anymore.'

I feel the weight of his wings press heavily on my shoulders, *"You will always need me,"* he hisses, angry in my ear and sends a pain through my heart. I ignore the spike of pain and fear and grip the side of Santi's leather jacket tighter, clinging to him and my desire for life.

"You ready?" He prods as a couple of bikes come up alongside us. My heart beat slows. Can I really do this? Can I leave Death behind and race towards a future? Santi laughs at my shaky nod and gives a mocking glare at me as I grip on even tighter. Here I go.

11

DEATH'S SACRIFICE

The loud crack of the starting shot echoes over the sounds of the bikes and the air fills with the rumble of engines as we speed off the beaten path. I hold onto Santi's back with even more adrenaline coursing through my veins than when I had the gun to my head as we weave through traffic. A wave of other racers follow behind us. My chin clutches as I grit my teeth. The wind rips through my hair just as my blood shoots through my veins. Is this what it's like to be so close to death but still so alive? The thought of death brings his presence close to me again and I feel his wings on my back, his breath against my ear, *"feeling awfully brave for a girl who is being so greedy, Lucia"* Death mutters against my skin, *"Why are you always chasing the love of others when you should know by now that we need no one else?"* Between my arms, I feel Santi's body tense and lean in preparation for the coming turn. *"Remember,"* my jealous lover whispers, *"you knew what would happen."* Death presses against my throat.

"Wait, Santi," The blaring lights of an eighteen-wheeler heading straight for us blind my sight and cuts off the rest of my warning. I inhale deeply and the world becomes a cloudy haze around me. I embrace the impact. Death is holding me up. Flashes of fire and smoke fill my vision as I hover over my body. From the sweet caresses down my back at night. To the soft whispers in my ears. Every heartbeat I take is like a barrier between Death and I. My heart's beating is the only symphony playing between me and my lover, protector ,and friend.

Now he is pulling me towards him into his grasp, promising me that there won't be another tomorrow. His embrace around my back feels like it did the night my parents died, with the small coat shrouding over my shoulders in the closet that I hid in. Death is the only thing consistent in my life from one foster home to another. He is always there. I still always miss him.

I tightly embrace the leather jacket over my shoulders. "Papi...How I long to be with you." That timid smile that greeted me with a tender embrace every time he came home from working. He was a mechanic, and worked hard with his hands. Mama filled the house with the aroma of every spice imaginable. Instead of the warmth of my home, I lay here. I clung to my jacket in my closet. The only comfort in the moment as I heard the mumbling of their voices. I knew something was off. Otherwise, Mom wouldn't have told me to go in here. There was something completely shielding me that day. A presence I never knew. Then came the final bang that brought it all upon me. The haunting reality that they were gone forever. I dared not leave the closet after the loud noise. The neighbors had called to report the sound of gunfire. And then the friendly man found me, a sad smile on his face. He was the only salvation and light I had in that moment. I grasped onto his arms as he carried me through the house and to the back of his police car. The back of a police car became a home to me as much as any other in the days that followed.

The howling of wind brushing through my hair, and this light bruising on my skin from the cement skid marks that replaced my dad's embrace.The ground beneath me shakes as flashing lights hover around me. You're here to stay this time, right, Death? My body begins to weaken as my blood flows onto the ground and my beating heart slows. I wanted this at one point, didn't I? For my life to fade and to be as close to Death as I could. And he's here now, a dark mass swirling above my body. I turn to see him. A pair of majestic black wings surrounds me. Am I flying? Is this what happens when we die?

"You are with me now." His voice consoles me. I wince to see Santi is being held by a pair of wings as well, his lifeless body

hanging on them, not only on the ground but completely whole and hovering in the air like mine.

"SANTI!" I shout. Nothing, no response. Why can't he hear me? A dark cloud comes over and consumes him. The wings that I know and am so fond of cover him.

"You want to be with me? I will take you to a new place." Death's voice rings through me, and I fly higher, among the sky lights of the city. The cold air trickles through my body. Why am I still here ,but Santi is gone?

"She's here, she's still here." A male voice yells out. There's a pulsing of my heartbeat, and a low hum of sounds begins to consume me. I gasp as rough, ragged hands pound against my chest. My eyes open up to the night sky. But this time I am not flying in it. The stars that surrounded Santi are barely visible. I am on the ground with the hard cement against my back. The feeling of pins and needles radiates throughout my body.

I look up to a masked figure. Brown hair, and then I see him. The skull, a scythe, and a hovering figure over him. My eyes dart completely open. Death, you're here. I turn, and I see the blood, the aftermath of Death's pursuit. Santi's face is unrecognizable on the ground beside me.

"No!" I scream. "No, he can't!" My body jolts with the electricity pulsing through my chest. The cold of hands and metal poke and prod, forcing life back into my body. I can't. I won't.

"Death," I pray, "please take me instead. I am yours, Death. I love you. Please take me." My eyes roll back and my body convulses. The faint beating of my heart echoes in my ears. This heart, it beats for you, Death. You can have it. It's the symphony of my life, slowly fading away and given to you completely. I feel the weight of my body go lax and the distant shouts, 'We're losing her.' The beating of them pressing against my chest grows harder, but I am in the sky again. Santi is before me with Death's wings holding us both up. I don't want to let him go. His face has the paint of death across it and a look of confusion.

He reaches for me. "Lucia?"

"You would give yourself for him?" Death whispers in my ear. *"Give yourself to me? This trade is forever. You can't take it back."* I turn to Death beside me, holding me in the air, and then at Santi. His eyes soulfully looking into mine.

I grind my teeth and turn to him with a nod. Giving in to Death has always been my fate; at least now, I know it will be worth something. "Death, you can have me. Just give him his life."

This is the moment I give in to his love. His obsession. The wings that have held me up to this point. That voice and whisper that has always romanced me. I don't know if this is love, but it's something I've never been able to escape. Whether it is from heaven or hell, I've never known. This is my death's romance.

The black wings that are choking around Santi's body slowly let go. I see a flash of them hovering around his body. "He has a pulse."

A man yells and several more people rush over to him and lift him from the ground.

Death's soft wings brush across my chest as he holds me up in the sky. I turn to the flaming skull. The flames begin to dance around my body, in a swirling oblivion just like when his wings covered me. Then the fire consumes me.

12

Death's Romance

Dried, dead leaves crinkle under my footsteps. The silent trail that comes with a wintry graveyard. No snow, just the cold air that glides across your neck like the chill of Death, reminding me that he is still there. And he had taken her.

I pick up the small candle left over from that night. The last time she breathed onto my chest, and reminded me of the life she gave me. Though that breath from her is silent now, it still brings life into the flame that is in me. It was a flame that wouldn't stop burning, until the day that I am taken by her lover, Death, too. I glide my hand across the stone.

"For you, Luce." I place the bouquet of marigolds on the ground that now has her in its clutches. "One step, one day at a time. I'll race for you, Lucia.... until I find myself in your arms again."

Tears streak my cheeks, running the white and black paint across my face. If only I could bring her back. I turn to the helmet on my bike, adjusting it to the frame of my chin. I don't wipe away the tears as they could trail my face in place of her soft kisses.

My bike's tires meet the pavement, that lead me to the race. A loud cheer follows me as I start revving my engine and my heart beats faster.

"Take me on your wings, Lucia." I pray and kiss her rosary hanging below my chest. My only remembrance of her besides my pain.

I have this life ahead of me because of her. There is the reminder as well that I will have Death ahead of me, too. As my body decays, day by day. Lucia's life reminds me there is promise for tomorrow's sunrise. We are gifted each moment. We must hold onto our youth, but as that fades, each wrinkle across your skin is a kiss from Death. It's a reminder that we are ultimately in his hands. All must pass through him. All must eventually succumb to his call. This life is not just a story, it is Death's slow romance.

13

DEATH'S LAST WORDS

Hell is an eternal fire. One that consumes you. I thought I had given in to each impulse. But the one I reserved. The one that I had not fallen into yet .The one that would send me to an eternal fire...was you, Lucia.

Acknowledgments:

My friend Rachel, for your wonderful editing dedication and friendship.

My Friend Eric Gustafson , for your edits , encouragement and support.

Book cover art by Artscandare and Marika Veil .

To the man who has become my Ride or Die , Nivik Ochoa.

Danielle Wolfe discovered her passion for vampire books as a teenager, sparking her dream of one day writing her own novel. Now she is a mother of two, alongside her husband, Nivik. Danielle brings her love for storytelling into works that bring light into the darkness of life. Her writing is driven by a mission to offer hope to those who are suffering. Her debut novel, Eternal Love, emerged from a deeply personal journey of finding light in the midst of her own darkness.

You can find out more about Danielle's upcoming books at DanielleWolfeBooks.com.